The Little Drummer Girl

Written by
Fe Serenity

Illustrated By: **Mark Ruben Abacajan**

Print information available on the last page

Rev. date: 12/02/2015

To order additional copies of this book, contact:
Xlibris
1-888-795-4274
www.Xlibris.com
Orders@Xlibris.com

Dedicated to Jesus

By: Fe Serenity

All Citlali wanted for the day of the Three Wise Men was a hug from her mom. Today was the 16th of December, the first day of the Posadas (re-enactment of Mary and Joseph finding a birthplace for baby Jesus). It was also the last Friday before Christmas break.

Citlali was playing Mary this year. She felt very privileged to play the role. She did her very best to not play around and listen to anyone talking to her. She sang and prayed when it was appropriate. At no time did anyone catch her just chit-chatting. She thought that she may receive a hug from her mom if she was super well-behaved during the Posadas.

It did not take much effort from her to be the best student. She received an 'A' on every assignment. She was awarded two prizes from the treasure box. One was for her grades and the other was for behavior. She chose two white pencils with red heart erasers.

Mrs. Peralta commented, "Citlali, I notice that you choose pencils or notepads over toys. Why is that?"

Citlali responded, "I like school and I love to write ... plus the hearts remind me of you and my dad."

"Oh really? In what way?"

"Both of you give me hugs. My dad also holds my hand. I just love that."

"Well, it is very important to feel loved and affection to be shown. You should know that these rewards are not as important as me hugging you."

"My mom does not hug me. She pushes me nearly every time I go near her. She says for me to go away."

"I wish I could be there for you when you feel rejected. I'm glad both your dad and I hug you." Mrs, Peralta gave her an appropriate hug.

Citlali went back to her seat. Mrs. Peralta was right. All the rewards and materialism in the world do not matter if you don't feel loved. You need to develop relationships that show you are loved.

Citlali went home. She showed the rewards to her mom and explained to her why she received them. Her mom did not acknowledge anything. She ignored her comments completely, just as Citlali had imagined.

However, her mom had an idea when she saw the two pencils with hearts. She thought of making a drum for Citlali. She made a drum out of a cylinder shaped object. She cut across it and put the lid on top. Then she cut the shape and size from red cloth to go around the drum. She sewed it together and then wrapped it around the cylinder. She then found some white ribbon and glued diagonals criss-crossing on the red drum. That would be her gift to match her two white pencils with red hearts. White was for purity and a narrow path to Jesus and red for love. She was going to give it to Citlali on January 6, the day of the Three Wise Men.

While on Christmas vacation, the Posadas continued at people's homes. Citlali enjoyed singing back and forth with the people who played the innkeepers. Praying repetively was boring, but nevertheless she did it to fulfill her role.

On December the 24th, the day of the "Acostada", the sleeping of baby Jesus, arrived. It was time to lay baby Jesus down and put him to sleep now that they found a place to stay, Citlali's home. Singing the lullabies to put baby Jesus to sleep gave Citlali the chills.

"Al cantar alba del día, nació el Niño Emanuelito, cantemos con alegría, a la rru Niño chiquito, Niñito Dios" ("At the break of dawn, little Emanuel was born, let us sing with joy, rock a bye little Boy, little Boy Jesus") just rung beautifully in her head.

She especially loved the sparkling of the twinkling lights. That night she fell asleep happily because of all the caring and nurturing that was shown to baby Jesus.

Days passed. Citlali was really missing her teacher. She liked the comments and praises she gave her. She loved to be acknowledged for her outstanding behavior and achievements.

Dad was working late, as usual. It seemed like eternity for his arrival; Citlali would stand and gaze out the window—sometimes in tears. When he finally arrived, Citlali desperately ran to receive his hugs. She was quick to take off his boots from his hard day's work.

Finally, school begun. Citlali ran to see her teacher. Mrs. Peralta gave Citlali her usual comfortable hug. Citlali felt very self-conscious because she was wearing the pants that had a hole on her knee area. She did not celebrate Christmas on the same day that her peers did, so she did not receive any new pants.

January 6th arrived; it represented the day of the Three Wise Men's visitation to baby Jesus. It was also time for the "levantada", the wakening and getting up of baby Jesus. Citlali's mom had knitted the clothes for Him. The godparents dressed baby Jesus and sat him up on a tiny chair.

Citlali took the drum that her mom gave her. She absolutely loved it! Her mom suggested for her to use the two pencils with the hearts to beat it. Once the Three Wise Men gave baby Jesus frankincense, myrrh, and gold and as soon as the group of people finished dressing and singing to baby Jesus; Citlali began to sing and beat her drum.

"I do not know what to do about her love, rum-pum-pum-pum

All I want from her is a hug, rum-pum-pum-pum

All I have to give is myself and my love, rum-pum-pum-pum"

Baby Jesus, I want to give you a hug, rum-pum-pum-pum, rum-pum-pum-pum, rum-pum-pum"

Citlali took off her drum that her mother had given her for the day of the Three Wise Men. She also took off the heart pencils that her teacher had given her. She kneeled in front of the manger and gave baby Jesus a kiss on his foot.

She began to cry and told baby Jesus, "I only have this drum and pencils to give you; I love you baby Jesus".

While Citlali was there, kneeling, an amazing thing happened. All of a sudden, she saw baby Jesus in her arms, The guests and Citlali were surprised! How could this happen? Baby Jesus was being rocked by Citlali. Both Citlali and her mother were in tears. When baby Jesus disappeared, the first person to give her an unforgettable hug was her mom. Citlali was the happiest she had ever been! Her dad was next and then everyone just began hugging each other.

From that day forward, Citlali's relationship with her mother flourished.

Afterwards, everyone celebrated with eating tamales, drinking champurrado, cutting and eating of the "rosca" (bread similar to Mardi Gras bread). Everyone took a turn cutting a piece. The person who cut the piece with the plastic baby Jesus in it was the one who was going to host the following year.

Finally, to end the night, the godparents gave each child a bag of goodies. The goodies included an orange, an apple, and Mexican candy (tamarind, etc.)

Printed in Great Britain
by Amazon

30849012R00016

Printed in Great Britain
by Amazon

25214503R00021